No. 1

Appledore
ARGOSY

Silk, Satin and
a Goodnight Kiss

Typeset by Jonathan Downes,
Cover and Layout by SPiderKaT for CFZ Communications
Using Microsoft Word 2000, Microsoft Publisher 2000, Adobe Photoshop CS.

First published in Great Britain by CFZ Press

**Appledore Argosy
Myrtle Cottage
Woolsery
Bideford
North Devon
EX39 5QR**

ISBN: 978-1-909488-61-8

The Game's Afoot...

Dear Friends,

Firstly I should like to thank you for picking up this very first copy of *The Appledore Argosy* and I hope that you shall be staying with us through future issues for a very long time. In doing so you have added a small but significant note to the history of short story publishing.

The original *Argosy* magazine was around for nearly one hundred years until, we were told, that the market for short stories had died. Beaten to death by half hour shows on television, perhaps?

However, for many of us the short story was the lubrication which so gently eased us into developing a taste for - or even an addiction to - literature in all its forms. Apart from resurrecting a love of the genre, the aim of this new magazine is to provide a platform from which unknown or little known Westcountry authors can display their wares to the wider world.

The lands surrounding the Torridge Estuary, and Appledore in particular, are particularly rich in literary talent, and - indeed - always have been. Authors like Rudyard Kipling, Rosemary Sutcliffe, Henry Williamson, Michael Morpurgo, and Charles Kingsley drew upon the genius loci of the region, but also enriched it by doing so. The psychogeographers would say that there is something in the DNA of the area which encourages this spiritual and artistic two way traffic, and this is something that this magazine is here to celebrate, support and encourage.

If you like, love or loathe our magazine please drop us a line or two for publication on the letters page of future issues.

Once again, please stay in touch.

Jim Jackson
Contents Editor

troubleshooter2000@live.co.uk

This first issue of *Appledore Argosy* is respectfully dedicated to Rudyard Kipling, who spent his school years at the United Services College, Westward Ho!

Contents

THINGS THAT GO BUMP IN THE NIGHT
by
Jim Jackson

On the far side of town a train rattled over wet points taking the last of the day's workers home in the hugga-mugga smoky atmosphere of its second class carriages. Its dim orange lights were just bright enough to read damp newspapers by, and its windows grey with condensation.

On the dark river tug boats hooted through the foggy air like melancholic territorial owls, and rain pattered against the back bedroom window of 43 Trafalgar Terrace, tucked away behind the streets, which were behind the streets, which ran between Camberwell and Peckham.

Straining his eyes in the darkness, Billy Deacon stared at the curtained window, lighter perhaps by half a degree than the room itself. A small room it was. A room dominated by a towering wardrobe built perhaps by giants for trolls and goblins to hide in, or so he believed. A board creaked, as boards in old houses do when settling down for the night. If that were not enough to chill the soul, there was something evil, something shapeless and dark between the curtains and the window. The harder he stared, the more he became convinced that it was moving. Slowly, so very slowly, it moved; agonisingly slowly with diabolic cunning so as not to be noticed. If he even so much as blinked it would appear as if it had never moved at all.

He bit his lip, fear mounting with every heartbeat. His heart was racing like a train now. He could hear it through his pillow. Drummers in the dark heart of Africa never sent such messages loaded with doom and foreboding. He tried not to give in to his fear and bit his lip harder until tears registered their presence. Soon his bladder would betray him for the coward he knew himself to be. He held on, but only just. A long drawn out second later his nerve broke, and he began to cry, and cry and cry and cry.

"There he goes again. Go and see to him."

"It's your turn. All he wants is a cuddle from his mummy."

"Well his mummy has to take his little sister to the clinic in the morning, you go. It's only another nightmare."

"Look Alice. Oh bloody hell, all right. Your feet are like ice, I'll go. No need to push. Oh bloody slippers."

"All right. All right, Daddy's here."

With the arrival of his father, the bringer of electric light, his heart returned to its normal routine rhythm.

"Another nightmare I suppose. What is it this time? Spacemen or ghosts?"

"There, Daddy. There behind the curtains."

And behind the curtains when pulled back? Nothing.

"There is nothing there Billy. There is nothing there in the dark that wasn't there when the light was on. See?"

Then to prove the point he switched the light on and off and on and off a few times but he could tell from his son's expression that logic was not going to be the route of the child's enlightenment.

"Look Billy, Mummy and I can't always be getting up every time you have a bad dream. You're a big boy now, how old? Nearly six. So this calls for drastic action. You know what I am going to do? I am going to ask two of my very best friends to stay here in your room with you. How about that? To be here with you whilst you sleep and see that you come to no harm."

Billy wasn't at all sure that he liked the idea of sharing a room. After all, having had the baby's cot here for just a few nights had not worked out at all well. He shook his head, but before he could articulate his protest his father continued.

"Oh you'll like them. They are two famous warriors. I have known them for, oh donkeys' years and because you are my little boy, and they owe me a favour, you can call on them at any time to come to your aid, at any time night or day. Their names are Courage and Imagination. Now Courage is a big strong chap, much bigger than me and wears a suit of blue steel armour. Arrows, knives, even bullets just bounce off. Nothing can touch him. He has this great big shield called Patience and a huge broadsword called Justice. Not even the most evil-evil bad men can beat him in a fight. Just can't be done. Stronger than Superman he is and smarter than, ummmm er Robin Hood."

"Don't believe you. Don't exist."

"He does too. Just close your eyes and you can see him standing guard over all of us. You, me, Mummy and baby Chrissie."

He could tell by the tightly closed eyes and the grim smile that a film was running inside Billy's little head. The blue eyes opened suddenly. "Tell me about Imagination. Tell me about him."

"Well for a start it's not a him its a her."

"A girl!"

"Yes a girl."

"Girls can't fight."

"This one is different. She doesn't have to fight - she has special powers."

"Please Daddy tell me about her too. Is she pretty?"

"Oh yes, very pretty."

"Is she as pretty as mummy?"

"Oh yes, much more pretty than mummy. Smarter too. She wears a long, thin silk dress which is sometimes grey and sometimes red when she gets cross, and sometimes black and then she can banish, with a snap of her fingers or a wave of the little white hand, even the most horrible evil spirits or bogey men. You know the sort of thing; the ones, like the thing you thought was hiding behind the curtains tonight. They all are just a bit silly, but they can't hurt you, not ever. Just keep you awake sometimes. If they do all you have to do is call up Imagination, and she will send them packing double quick, you see if they don't hop it smartish. No matter how strong they think they are, and no matter how strong you think they are, Imagination is even stronger so you need never be frightened ever again. With Courage and Imagination here beside you in you room, Mummy and me in the next room. With Uncle Colin and the whole of the Metropolitan Police Force clomping up and down outside with their truncheons and great big hobnailed boots. With an enormous army, navy and air force guarding us with guns and tanks and stuff, what on earth could you possibly have to worry about that might make a big boy like you cry?

"Now off you go to sleep. Oh you are asleep. Shagged out by all that howling I expect. Goodnight dear boy. I love you, you little bugger, and I have to face Mr Cattamole of human resources at 9:00 tomorrow. All nonsense really, just because of a bit of a prank in the stationary cupboard."
As he stood up to return to his own bed he saw his wife framed in the doorway.

"Oh Jimmy," she said. "What wonderful things to say to the child. You old softie – come here."

With that, she gave him a long tender kiss on the lips. Then suddenly her mood changed abruptly, as it will with women from time to time, and she stepped back. A cat with its tail caught in a slamming washing machine door would no doubt have displayed similar emotions upon its features at the sudden change in its personal circumstances.

"What was it you were getting up to in the stationary cupboard and with whom?"

"And who exactly did you have in mind that wears thin, silk dresses and has such slender lily-white hands, and is so very much prettier and so much smarter than dull, ugly, stupid old mummy? Answer me that then you, you -----."

He could tell she was cross.

Swiftly, with the speed of a bounding lion Courage leapt to his rescue with his great sword and shield, deftly turning aside the deadly lance point of suspicion.

"No-one dear," he replied. "It's just Imagination."

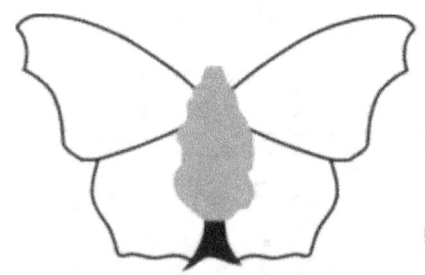

'Irsha Street' by Barrie Payne

Butterfly
Conservation

Saving butterflies, moths and our environment

https://butterfly-conservation.org/

A Winter's Night on Irsha Street.
by
Richard Small

Comfortingly back home in my contemporary kitchen, doors locked tight and electric lights all on, ... I sit with my elbows resting on my old pine table, its enduring strength a reassuring prop to my insecurities. My much loved table, despite its many sufferings, it has stood the test of time. I feel the warmth from the log fire sending out its comforting glow across the room, the burning wood crackling a song of the forest, accompanied by a hushed but harmonious howling as air is drawn through small iron vents. Both the table and fire somehow seem to connect me to the past, with happy memories of days that were for me perhaps not as durable. I pick up a note book and begin to write for you, though my senses are still somewhat puzzled by the events that occurred during a visit I made earlier that evening to a little place called Irsha Street.

Irsha, almost a place that time has forgotten, was a quaint little street in a remote old fishing village. Irsha is long and narrow, with only a car width road and no pavements; many small alley ways disappear left and right into a darkness that has dwelled for centuries between the houses, some paths disappear inland towards the hill and some out towards the sea. The houses on one side of Irsha stand elevated from the sea on a cliff like stone sea wall. Lower down, even closer to the sea, once stood other old seafarer's houses, but these had failed to endure tide and time and stand no more; no trace remains, as if they never were.

As I write this, something is telling me that I am not entirely alone in this seemingly empty kitchen, something gently touches the crown of my head as if to say they know what I am doing, ... perhaps a warning, but there is no sense of dread, not this time, just a presence that has joined me from where I know not and nor why.

In any event, alone or accompanied, I'll still share with you of my visit.

"Call in for a cup of tea sometime," Joe had said.

So, on this wet winter's night, as occasional drizzle drifted here and there dropping gentle rain on the nearby rugged Devon coast, I thought it time I accepted his kind offer.

I left my car in the poorly lit and deserted quayside car park, put on my long black overcoat and adjusted my scarf and woolly hat against the damp. As I walked alongside the waterfront railings into the darkness towards Irsha, pinpoints of coloured light brightened the murk far across the bay; warnings to sailors of sandbars and rocks; sparkling beacons distant in a dark foreboding sea. As I entered Irsha Street the wind dropped and all became hushed, even my shoes on the tarmac were strangely silent, as were the many houses I passed on either side. The street itself was deserted; and seemingly so were most of the houses, only one or two showed a light, and even then no one was to be seen through the glass, I didn't like to peer inside for fear of someone looking out only to be disturbed by such ill mannered intrusion.

Directions and landmarks I'd been given soon led me to the house I sought; it was pleasantly easy to find in fact.

It was dark in Irsha except for the few dim street lights that sporadically lit the narrow roadway; a roadway wet from earlier rain that evening. There was a light on in the house and I could clearly see through the window I had found the right place; my host was sitting in a large chair in the far left corner of what appeared surprisingly to be quite a large room. I soon found the door, and knocked.

I didn't have to wait long before the door opened and a smiling face greeted me.

"Come on in," Joe said, "come on through."

I bowed my head through the low doorway and entered.

Once inside, I found the house was much larger than I had anticipated, I previously thought that they were all small two up two down cottages along Irsha. As is so often the case, what we think we see isn't what we think it is. There's many a surprise in life for us all about what we thought we saw. The entrance lobby and first room through which we walked was unlit, except for light coming through an opening to the next room, but I could still see the beamed ceiling, tasteful furniture and paintings. Underfoot I felt the cold and uneven flags of the 16th Century stone floor. We moved through the opening into a similarly presented room. My host, a worldly wise, stocky and affable man of some years was talking to someone that I could not see. It all became clear as he ushered me through a low opening to yet more rooms at the back and there was the lady of the house, the partner to his conversation, quietly making tea. She was a pleasantly positive and talkative lady who invited me to remove my coat and sit a while and 'did I want sugar in my tea'?

'That's a relief,' I thought, at least he's not talking to imaginary people; or worse still, something else of which my mind would rather stay in ignorance.

It was a large and interesting back room, with a central inglenook fireplace complete with old ironmongery for hanging meat and cooking pots. All around were misshapen ancient walls, on which paintings of seascapes and sailing ships hung as testimony to a maritime past, and floors that leaned this way and that in no particular order. As my tea slowly went cold in my hands my host's conversation continued absorbingly, with tales of smugglers, murders, secret tunnels and of footsteps heard crossing the wooden floors of the empty rooms above. Joe spoke quietly of these things in the manner of a man that knew the truth of this world.

Once an old inn, both the building and its contents smacked of another age. It was almost as though I had gone back in time, as though the energy left by the past was still present and willing to show itself. The conversation led me to sense that I too might 'see', 'hear' or 'feel' the past. After tea I was shown around the labyrinth of rooms and stairs of all shapes in which many a hiding place could remain a secret for all times. I stood on steps where once stood the murdered excise officer and I walked the floor over which many a contraband barrel had rolled, I looked to the walls and floors, beyond which lay secret places and hidden history, in part I felt that my soul saw more than my eyes.

How often have we glimpsed something from the corner of our eye but when we look again there is nothing there ... or was there? The child that plays with imaginary friends, or sees something in the night, is soon put right by the knowing and fearful adult. ..... "best not to look ... no, no, don't look, ... don't tell me any more ... there's nothing there .... Go to sleep, close your eyes."

Whose eyes is it that were really closed?

Another cup of tea and the invisible hours had passed us by, as though they never were ....

I picked up my nearly drunk tea ... the cup was cold to my touch ......"Gosh, is that the time?" I said, glancing at the digital watch on my wrist, "I really must be away home and leave you in peace; thank you so much for your timeless hospitality, most interesting," ... and, reflecting upon their revelations, thinking privately, 'and almost beyond belief too'.

I bid farewell and re-crossed the 16th Century stones to the door with Joe, the gentleman of the house. He too seemed timeless, as though he were part of the fabric of the old Inn himself, at one with the hostelry, attuned to the heartbeat of the house that held so many secrets.

Buttoning my long dark overcoat it seemed to fit me better than when I'd arrived, I somehow felt taller, more comfortable and strong, as though younger now, almost like being someone else. I stepped into the rain damped narrow street, the old Inn door closing quietly behind me.

I began a silent, contemplative walk eastwards along the hushed and still deserted Irsha. My mind wandered to the events of the evening, then I glimpsed something from the corner of my eye; something large that loomed out of the darkness. My eyes slowly accustomed to the night and a faint breeze carried the smell of salt air to my nostrils and the creaking of timbers and rigging to my ears .... as the darkness was eased apart by shifting clouds a faint moonlight revealed an ancient ship of two masts riding newly at anchor in the deep water channel, rolling so gently in harmony with the tireless estuary waves, her sails furled, ... I thought I saw movement on deck, thought I saw the swing of the hurricane lamp, ... and then nature drew its curtain of clouds once more to hide the moon and I was left with a darkness within a darkness and the sound of water lapping the rocks. A previously unknown knowing came in to my head, she was a Brigantine, yes, that's what she was, a Brigantine, two masted and shallow draft .... and not long home from sea too.

If she was truly there or not, now I cannot say, but that night I knew exactly where she was, how tall, how rigged and all such detail that could be seen and told.

All was made more real by the clearly audible, slow soporific swoosh of gentle waves lapping the shore in slow rhythm, with the pauses between almost as though the sea were holding its breath.

As I passed by the little slipway I sensed three men, short and stocky, wearing mufflers and caps, heaving their fully laden row boat further up the stone slip, for the tide was still not yet passed to the ebb. I did not linger to watch, but somehow intuition told me what they were doing; contraband. How thankful I was now that I had left the house when I did, this was no place for the faint hearted and those men would not be best pleased to be discovered.

The spectre of a long gone past began to haunt Irsha, and I edged nearer the middle of the empty street for safety. I walked on quietly not wishing to disturb what was happening, yet slightly fearful and knowing I could no longer turn back, it was as if I had entered the sorcerer's cave and now fear to wake him.

Irsha is long and narrow but this night it seemed ever more so, time seemed confused in some way, the street, like time, never seeming to end. Then something walked alongside me, I became aware of two men, who though strongly built seemed of a desperately nervous disposition; their nailed boots trod not on tarmac but on rutted stones and there was a fleeting whiff of rotting vegetation and sewage in the air as if it lay in the street. They walked in a greater darkness than I. It would appear that the men did not see me, or if they did I meant nothing to them. Nothing I saw seemed to see me, a cloak of timely invisibility covered me, though at times I feared it would not.

I became aware of the untidy ramshackle quay side with its frames, boxes and nets and the river beyond as though there were now no houses between me and they.

I walked on and on, passing some small houses that seemed no more than pauper's hovels and into one of which both men vanished. It was as though they never were, except that the sound of their voices lingered on, it was the last thing to pass ... a curse it was, 'twas press gangs working the town that they cursed, ... then their voices followed them into their greater silence, and Irsha was quiet again.

Driven by an unexpected and transient gust of wind some smoke drifted across the street; the smell of wood smoke filled the air and my now heightened senses. I moved on, still slow and in a silence, sensing, as I passed by, places born of centuries past itself, the shivers, the hunger, the fear, a sense of little expectation from life but to survive, a sense of those waiting in vain but always in hope of a loved son's return from the sea.

I walked out of Irsha and towards the Church and its graveyard. There, no doubt, we might find our ghosts' ageing bones but so often the poor can leave no markers except in our hearts. We may still be touched by their troubled spirits even today, if we did but take notice.

Somehow transformed by my journey into Irsha, words of noble poetry and stories of the soul sprang eagerly to mind and those words triggered feelings. Not unlike hearing songs or stories that can fill us all with feelings. Feelings as if we were still there, like when we were young; feelings that connect us to our own past and even to our own ancestors and a knowing what they must have done and felt …. For in part, we are them. In our mind we can belong to a different place and time … even if for a brief while, for a glimpse is all we need in order to 'know' ….. You must have been there yourself; you must have felt this in your own being sometime, somewhere. …….

Irsha was well behind me now and I carried only memories with me towards the live music that came from the local pub. To my left a glint of Moonlight, which had evaded the clouds, crossed the river to the street lights of Instow.

The pub was full of friendly people enjoying the warmth of drink and music, the bar was full of life. Warm applause greeted the rag tag and bobtail group of musicians as the song ended, leaving me with residual feelings ….. feelings that were trapped briefly in time past …. Once again I felt the strength of my youth and the courage of my forebears, my mind had transcended time and distance if only for a while. I ordered a Guinness from the bar and I reflected on an old saying, 'if the end is part of the story, then death is a part of living,' …. Perhaps we too will 'live on' somehow too. …..

"The end of anything is never a stopping point;
It is merely the doorway to new discoveries".

1069 AND ALL THAT

by

Nick Arnold

9 pm GMT, Friday 26th June 1069 – northern Devon

The battle was over. As the long June evening faded into night the surviving raiders left their lines and headed towards their ships. Many of them were wounded and limping, supported on spears or by their friends. Both sides had lost many men and were totally exhausted after hours of fighting. The victorious army held their ground and watched over a darkening field thickly strewn with corpses. There would be no pursuit.

The story of the battle begins in January 1068. At the time no Norman had ventured into southwest England and apparently inspired by Gytha the indomitable and wealthy mother of the slain King Harold, Exeter chose to defy King William. After an eighteen day siege William took the city and Gytha fled – but her cause was not lost. King Harold had sons and in May they made their way to Ireland to seek the aid of King Dairmait, the High King.

The Irish King had a history of supplying disaffected English nobles with men and ships for profitable raids. In 1052 he provided Harold and his brother, Leofwine with a small fleet when their family was exiled from England. In 1068 he provided Harold's sons – Godwine, Edmund and perhaps Magnus with 52 Irish longships.

In June they raided the Bristol area. They defeated an army of local levies at Bleadon and plundered the coasts of southwest England. Harold's sons returned to England in 1069, but this time the Normans were waiting.

On this fateful day in June 1069, the raiders landed around 9 am, beaching at least 64 longships, and many of the raiders raced off to plunder the area. There is an image of plundering in the Bayeux Tapestry and we can imagine something similar in 1069. The raiders were probably unarmoured and may not have carried shields. They had to be mobile to catch livestock and people. The raiders were mostly from Dublin, which had the largest slave market in Western Europe, so it's likely that along with animals to slaughter and money, the raiders were after young people to sell.

What they didn't know was that Brian, King William's Breton second cousin,

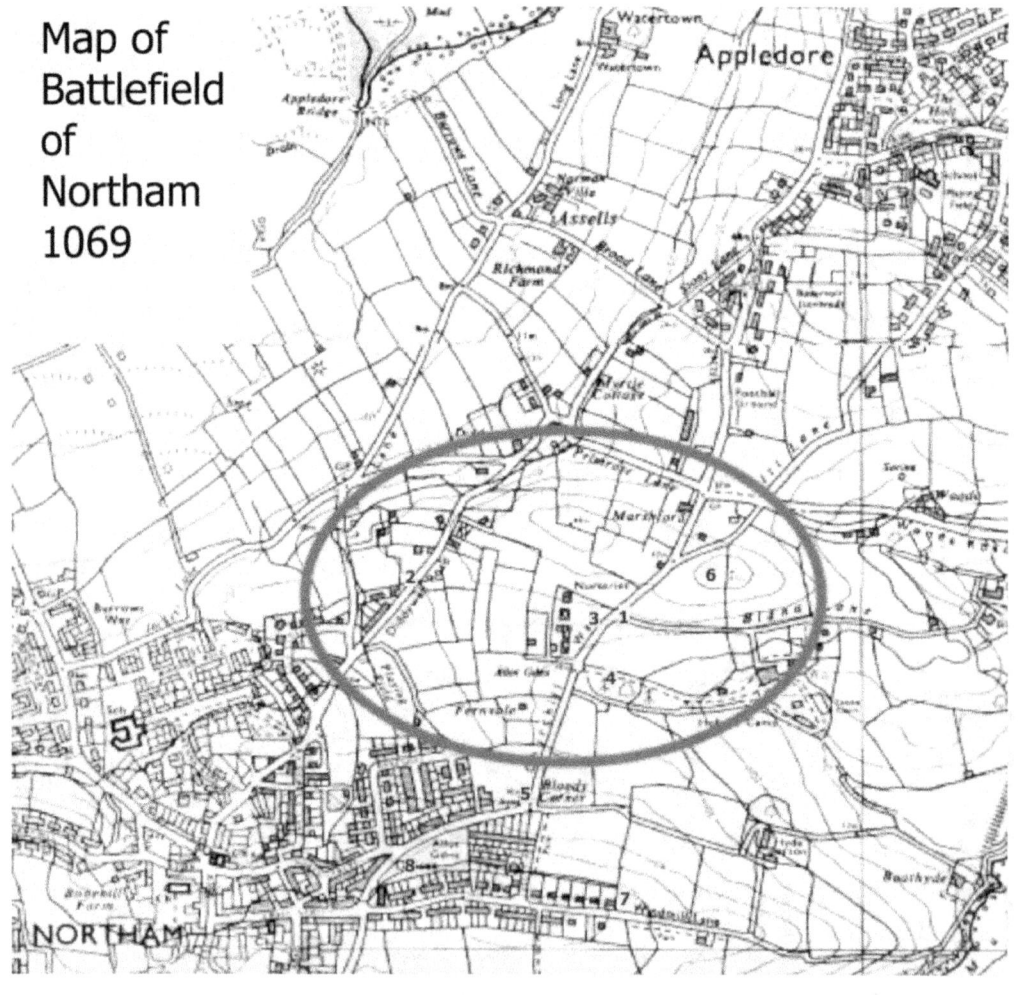

Map of
Battlefield
of
Northam
1069

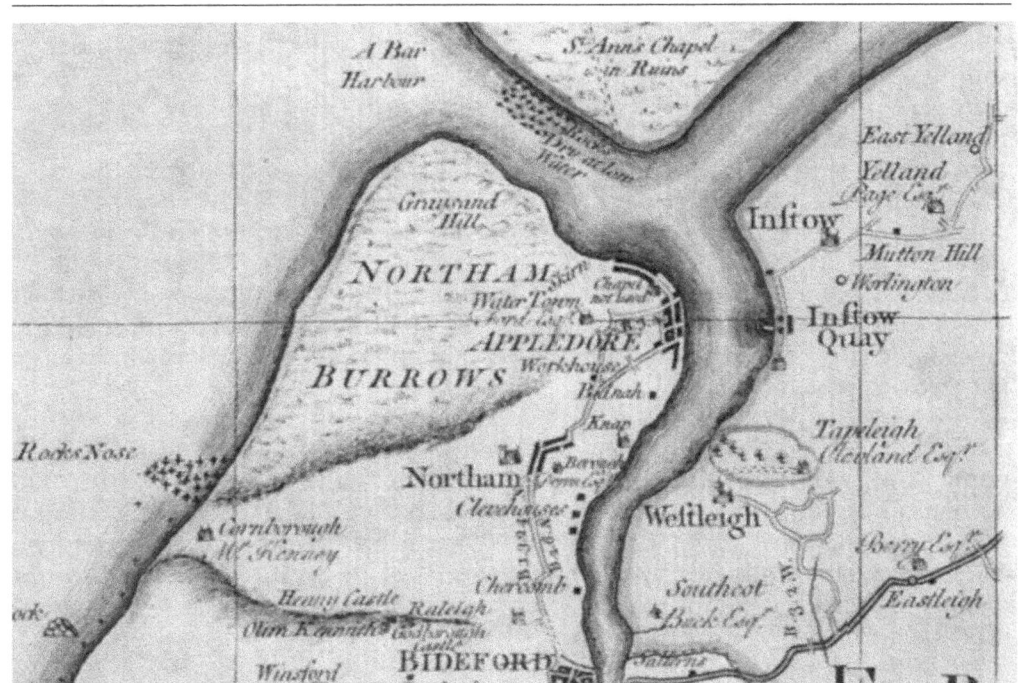

awaited them with a force of Bretons, Normans and Devon levies. We don't know who tipped Brian off about the raid, but it's possible that merchants or spies brought the news from Ireland. Brian's army attacked and put the plunderers to flight. But escape was impossible. The tide had receded – their ships were stranded on the gravelly yellow sand. They were trapped.

On the way to their ships the raiders formed a shield wall and prepared to fight or die. They had no other choice – they had to hold on until the tide came in. Brian's army attacked and the two armies fought a ghastly re-match of Hastings. There were veterans of the 1066 battle on both sides and their tactics and weapons were unchanged.

Once again Harold's family lost – this time 1,700 warriors died including many of their leaders, although Harold's sons escaped. No doubt Brian's force suffered heavy losses too although we have no figure. Assuredly this was the bloodiest battle after Hastings – and yet for almost one thousand years the battlefield and its significance have been lost … until today.

Amongst landscape historians William George Hoskins is a legendary figure – a Professor of Economic History at Oxford and the founder of their discipline. In 1954 he published a history of Devon in which he noted, rather casually, that a place named 'Bloody Corner' in the Parish of Northam could be the site of the 1069 battle. Other writers took up the suggestion but no-one offered any evidence.

It's a common problem. Early medieval battlefields are notoriously elusive – sources are usually vague or non-existent and archaeology rarely survives. But in the case of the 1069 battle there *is* evidence. It's just that until now no-one has troubled to look for it, let alone join up the dots.

The 1069 battle was reported in Version D of the *Anglo-Saxon Chronicle* and separately by a Norman monk named William of Jumiéges and both accounts were expanded by later writers. The account by Jumiéges was apparently based on eyewitness testimony within weeks of the battle. Better still, this was a battle that was determined by tide times and civil dusk and both can be plotted with scientific precision and combined with historic geography to create a coherent narrative – a narrative supported by circumstantial evidence.

The *Chronicle* stated that the sons of Harold landed in the mouth of the Taw in north Devon. But there's a problem. In detective novels it's known as a 'red herring'. Twelfth century historian Orderic Vitalis located the landing at Exeter. It took me months to figure out how and why Orderic got it wrong, but in any case an earlier source known as *Quedam Exceptiones* makes it clear that the raiders *weren't* aiming for Exeter – and this from a writer who was well-informed about local affairs in Exeter.

Back in north Devon, we can be certain that the landing at 'the mouth of the Taw' took place at Appledore. Appledore was the only practical landing place in the estuary, it was in use in 1069 and it was even called 'Tawmouth'. What's more Appledore offered the only land route to the Cornish border - and according to *Quedam Exceptiones* this is precisely where the sons of Harold were heading.

The landing place can be checked another way – by comparing it to the known landing places of the 1068 raid. In that year the sons of Harold targeted royal lands and in 1069 Appledore was also royal land. It was part of the manor of Northam, one of a cluster of north Devon manors held by Queen Matilda, wife of the Conqueror. In 1068 the two known landing sites of Harold's sons adjoined lands held by clerics allied to their father. In 1069 yet another ally, Sihtric, Abbot of Tavistock held Abbotsham, next door to Northam. Assuming that medieval raiders were creatures of habit, it looks like Harold's sons were carrying on where they left off in 1068.

So the raiders landed in Appledore, but where did they do their plundering and where did the battle take place? According to William of Jumiéges the raiders plundered the people of the 'landholding' - and this can only mean the manor of Northam. In 1069 armies fanned out in different directions to plunder - so they couldn't have marched anywhere else.

In any case, they had no time to go anywhere else. Jumiéges adds that Brian attacked 'immediately' and according to the Chronicle this was a surprise attack.

1069
BATTLE ᚠf
NᚬRTHAM

©Kim Jones & Mary Myers

Ever since the ninth century, English armies had attacked sea raiders by surprise close to the coast and the Normans used the same tactic - so Brian's attack makes perfect sense.

Whilst we can't be certain where this attack took place - it is highly likely that it was around Northam village. In 1069 this is where most people lived, so it must have been the main target of plundering. What's more the landscape supports the Chronicle's account of a surprise attack. If you look at Northam village from the direction of Appledore, you will see that high ground blocks your view to the south. There is no way the raiders could have been seen by Brian's army before it attacked them.

It's easy to imagine Brian's Breton knights riding down the plunder-laden raiders. Naturally the raiders ran for their ships – where else could they go? And just as naturally most of them followed the road (the alternative was to run across a marsh.) The medieval route from Northam to Appledore was much where it is today – and *Quedam Exceptiones* places the battle between the first skirmish and the ships. The location is supported by the tide and dusk data for the likely date of the battle – Friday 26th June. The data shows that the battle must have been fought within a few minutes of Appledore and it so happens that the historic landscape offers the perfect site.

Surely such a lengthy battle of attrition would only have been possible in a defensive position that couldn't be outflanked. In 1069 the area of Bloody Corner was a ford across a marsh formed by the watershed of two streams and overlooked by a ridge. Today this area is

Picture courtesy Bill Wright Artist Illustrator - Appledore.

still called 'Marshford'. It's the only place where the battle would have been possible but even if I'm wrong – I can't be far wrong. The gap between Northam and Appledore isn't much larger than the battlefield of Stamford Bridge. In other words you can argue where the armies lined up but there can be no question about the area of the fighting.

Today most of the battlefield remains open land ready to inspire historians and future generations. But it is in danger of inappropriate development. The only question is whether the people of Northam can protect and cherish this area as an irreplaceable part of their shared heritage - as the people of Sussex cherish the battlefield of Hastings.

After the battle, Harold's sons returned to Ireland for what must have been an uncomfortable interview with King Dairmait. Later on, they may have sailed to Denmark where an Irish longship found in Roskilde fjord is a candidate for their vessel. Despite his victory, Brian's success was short-lived. In 1070 he left England - probably after a quarrel with his second cousin.

King William apparently forgot the 1069 battle but his queen didn't. Northam was her manor and she was very devout. The 1069 battle took place during the feast of a local saint martyred at Appledore and the saint's heavenly help had to be acknowledged. Perhaps this is why the Queen gave land in alms to the saint's former lay patron. Such a grant was unusual - the Queen made no other grants to English laymen. On her deathbed the Queen was vexed by God's disfavour towards her husband and she gave Northam to St Stephen's Abbey, Caen. The gift of Northam to an Abbey founded to benefit William's soul looks like atonement for the battle – think of William's gift of Battle Abbey in atonement for the slaughter of Hastings. In other words it was a spiritual bribe to regain God's favour for King William.

The Battle of Northam – as we may now call it – was more than an obscure skirmish deservedly lost in the mists of time. It was the largest, bloodiest battle after Hastings. It was truly a battle of nations, involving Irish and Norse warriors from Dublin, English retainers of King Harold, Breton and Norman knights and men from all over Devon.

For people in 1069, the Norman Conquest was a dynastic contest for the crown of England, and the final defeat of Harold's family marked the very climax of the struggle. The Battle of Hastings won William the crown but Northam set the seal on that victory and although its location was forgotten, the consequences of what happened on that fateful June day in 1069 have echoed down the centuries.

Strength Through Koi

Honorary Aryan (German: Ehrenarier) is a term from Nazi Germany; it was a status granted by the Bureau of Race Research to people who were not considered to be biologically part of the Aryan race as conceived by the Nazis, but were granted an "honorary" status of being part of that race, for example because their services were deemed valuable to the German economy.

Wikipedia – The Free Encyclopaedia

One of my favourite songwriters is a chap called Roy Harper. Sadly, he has had very little commercial success, and I think it is unlikely that anyone under the age of 35 (and quite a few readers over that age), will have actually heard of him. However, in a career which has lasted since 1964 he has recorded numerous albums of his idiosyncratic songs. One of my favourites is called *Loony on the bus*, in which he bemoans the fact that whenever he goes anywhere, and whatever he is doing, he has a tendency to become accosted by people ranging from the mildly eccentric to the certifiably insane who want to tell him their life story. I have always understood that particular song, because the same thing seems to happen to me with monotonous regularity.

In 2002 - as many readers may well be aware - I led an expedition to Martin-Mere nature reserve in Lancashire. We were in search of a giant fish which had been reportedly attacking waterfowl overwintering at the reserve. We found the fish, identified it, and then came home again. However, we were amazed at the enormous amount of interest that this - seemingly quite innocuous - story seemed to me garner within the pages of the British press. As a result of this, only a few days after we had come back to our base in Exeter, my colleague and friend Richard Freeman and I found ourselves back in Lancashire to make a live broadcast from the side of the lake on breakfast television.

This necessitated Richard and me travelling up there the day before.

We spent a the night at a hotel in Southport and as is our wont we spent most of the evening prior to the broadcast sitting cheerfully in the bar. We were reading an issue of *Koi Carp* magazine and drinking lager when an extraordinary pair of people approached us.

"Ere, you're the two lads who were chasing that bloody great fish?" said a small, wizened old man with an almost impenetrable Lancashire accent. He glared at us accusingly, as his companion - a young man with vicious eyes and a skinhead haircut stood just behind him, cleaning his fingernails with a fork that he had taken from the hostess trolley by the door. We gulped our beer and admitted that yes, indeed we were the people who had gone on a successful search for the monster of the Mere. "Well you found it, what's you doing back here again?" he asked in a slightly menacing manner. We explained about our imminent appointment with GMTV, and the atmosphere thawed somewhat. "You mind if we join you?" the younger one asked, but the way that he asked it was phrased so that it wasn't really a question. Neither Richard nor I actually wanted company - we were tired, and all we want to was to drink, talk nonsense, and then retire to our respective hotel rooms. However it appeared that we were not going to be able to get rid of this unpleasant pair without an overt act of hostility, so we gestured to them are to join us.

The younger of the two picked up my copy of *Koi Carp* magazine. "You interested in those big buggers?" he asked, and before I could answer him he continued " I gotta story for you".

He then recounted a story, which is quite possibly the strangest, and most bizarre

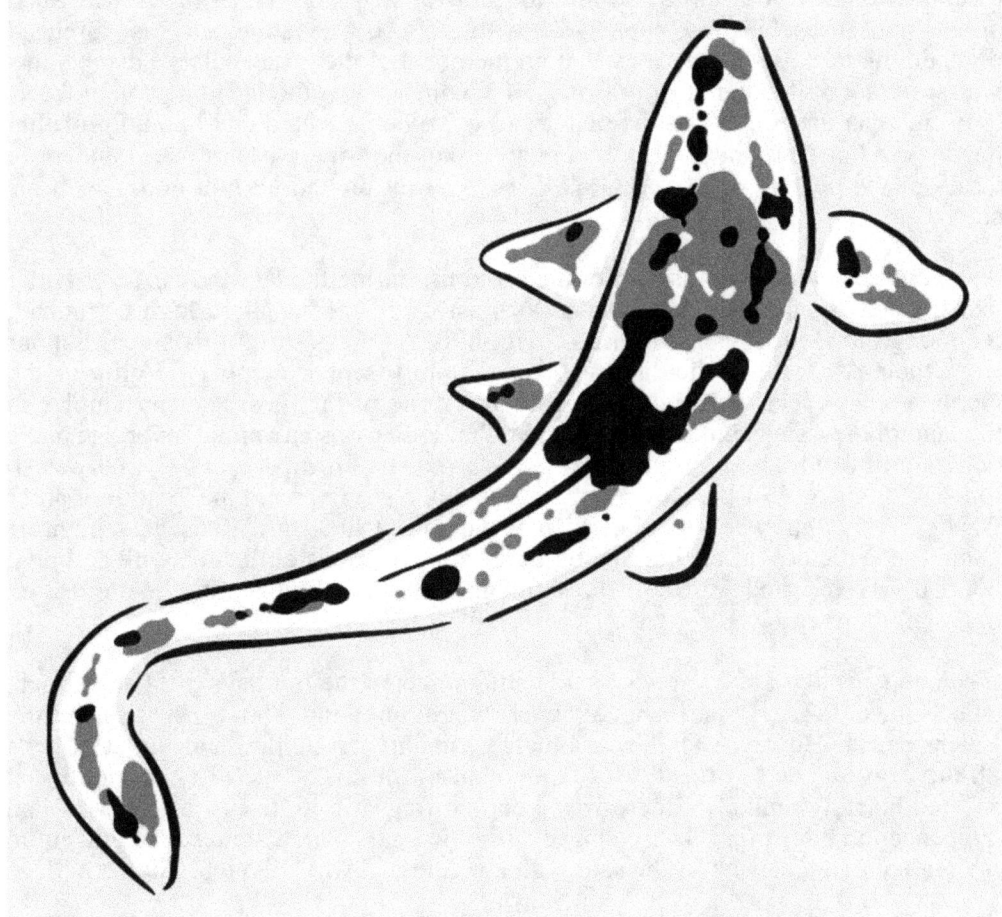

tale, which I have ever recounted in this column—and as regular readers will know that is saying something! I am repeating the story just as we were told it with no guarantees as to its veracity. All I would do is quote the old Latin - *vaverat lector* - let the reader beware!

The old man, whom - it must be said - looked even older once we could see him up close, claimed that before the second world war, as a young man, he had been a member of Sir Oswald Mosley's British Union of Fascists. When the organisation was declared illegal in 1940, alongside many other "blackshirts" he had been sent to the civilian internment camp on the Isle of Man. His brother, however (the younger man's grandfather), had - despite holding similar political views - been an NCO in the British Army and had fought his way through the European campaign, finally ending up with the first British Regiment to enter Berlin in 1945.

"What would you say to me if I told your that I knew where the Fuhrer's pet fish were?" he grunted at me in a combative, and slightly menacing manner. My first reaction would have been to tell him to go away and stop bothering us with such arrant nonsense, but his nephew - with an ACAB tattoo on his forehead proclaiming to those in the know that all members of the constabulary have parents who were not united in the Holy Bonds of Wedlock - was threatening enough for us to decide that discretion was the better part of valour. Richard and I could probably have taken him, but brawling in hotel bars is not the way to best impress either the lasses or the powers that be at GMTV, so we shut up and let him go on with his story.

Apparently, so our unpleasant informant told us, during the late 1930s Adolf Hitler had granted "honorary Aryan" status to most of all the Japanese high command, including the God Emperor himself - Hirohito. As a riposte to this signal honour from their Axis allies, the Japanese royal family sent a number of gifts to the German leader. These included koi carp from one of the most ancient temples in the land of the rising sun. It is well known that Hitler was an animal lover. He had a dog called `Goldi`, and in many ways was a sensitive man. Apparently, he was so touched by the gift of the Royal fish that he had a special pond made in the Führer Bunker. Although, when he realised that the end of the Third Reich was nigh, he committed suicide - after first having made similar provision for his wife and dog, his fish survived, and were somehow smuggled back to England by the unpleasant old man's brother.

It so happens, that I know a reasonable amount about the last days the Third Reich, and I have to say that I have never heard anything about pet fish in the Reichskanzel. However I knew about the sad fate of Goldie, and about Hitler's affinity towards and sympathy for nonhuman life forms, so despite the fact that it seemed horribly unlikely - there was a certain ring of truth to it. I asked what had happened to Hitler's fish. The younger of the two men glared at me. "I've got 'em in my garden pond, haven't I?" he said with a vicious scowl. Although, I didn't believe the story for a moment, I was interested enough to ask if it was possible for us to come and see them. After all, if the story is true, despite the historical importance of these fish they would be well over 70 years old, and would be an impressive sight.

However, they made it perfectly obvious that they were not going to accede to our request. Both Richard and I had long hair, and were obviously degenerates of the worst kind. These last survivors of the Third Reich had existed since 1945 in suburban Southport, and if their guardians had anything to do with it they would stay, in seclusion, for many more years to come. The unwarranted intrusion of people like us could only attract the wrath of left-wing activists who might harm the fish, or more realistically the military authorities who would want to impound them because of their undoubted historical and military interest. No, they were not prepared to tell us any more than they already had.

The bell for last orders rang, and we made our excuses and left. Was this extraordinary tale true? Could there be a valuable historical relic swimming peacefully in a pool in suburban Lancashire? Or were these two unpleasant characters just the latest manifestations of what Roy Harper meant when he sang "Why do I always find myself next to the loony on the bus?"

I doubt whether we will ever know the answer to either question.

Jon Downes

DOES DIGITISATION THREATEN DEMOCRACY?

''Or does democracy threaten
digitisation?''

This is a factual story discussed in the novel
'The Shanghai Incident' *regarding China and Russia.*

by

James Dalby

Before_discussing digitisation, I need to discuss codes and cyphers, as they are essential to the proliferation of the digital age in order to ensure our data is safe, and only available to those who should receive it.

A cypher is a method of sending plain text in code that is unintelligible to anyone but the recipient.

We know that Julius Caesar used cyphers to communicate between his legions, they were simple but effective at that time. The problem with a cypher is that if someone other than the recipient can break it, it is no longer any use.

Mary Queen of Scots used a cypher when communicating with members of the Babington plot, the problem was the cypher was given to her by a trusted friend, who was working for the enemy, the enemy being Walsingham our first real spy master. It cost her her life. The point here is if you are using a cypher; make sure you know where it comes from.

As time went on, the search for a safer cypher was important, as diplomatic secret reports needed to be passed between countries. Of course, we talk about secrecy, but nothing is really secret once more than one person has the same knowledge, but the idea is to ensure that only the people who should have the information, receive it, it being gibberish to others who should not.

The modern innovation for cyphers came from a Frenchman named Blaise de Vigenere who developed a table of 26 letters by 26 letters which enabled the use of 'keys'. This prevented a code breaker from finding similarities in the cypher text. A key incidentally could be a simple word. However, nowadays keys are often as long as the message making decryption much more difficult.

The Vigenere system was eventually compromised (broken), and the most publicised result was the breaking of the Zimmerman telegram by the British during World War 1, which brought the Americans into the war. In fact, the breaking of the cypher was only one of the machinations the British went through to ensure there was no suspicion that it was they who had deciphered it. It is possible that if Zimmerman himself had not confirmed that he had sent it, the telegram would not have had the same impact. The lesson here for anyone in the secrets business is, if you do not have to admit anything, keep quiet or deny it.

For those that don't know the Zimmerman story, it was sent to the President of Mexico by the German Foreign Office offering to support Mexico in cash and supplies to invade the USA and annex Texas, New Mexico and Arizona.

The next major innovation was invented by a German named Arthur Scherbius, and this is where we enter the machine age in cryptology. At first, the Germans were not interested in this machine which today we call the enigma, but the Poles were, and for this we were fortunate, but this is not relevant to this story.

After the Second World War, commercial companies were as keen as countries to have an unbreakable cypher that could be used by anyone who wanted to encrypt their data or financial transactions. This became critical when digitisation became available to the masses, which was from 1981 when the personal computer started to be freely available.

What was required was a method whereby the recipient did not need to hold the key, and this is where RSA came into being. RSA was invented by three Americans called Rivest, Shamir and Adleman who devised a method of being able to send a privately encrypted message, with the person at the other end being able to use a public key to decrypt it or vice versa. The basis of the system is the use of prime numbers. For those of you wanting to know exactly how it works, go to the following link: (doctrina.org/How-RSA-Works-With-Examples.html).

They became multi-millionaires as a result, but a British man, Clifford Cocks, who invented a similar process much earlier was not allowed to publish or patent his invention due the fact that he worked for GCHQ.

The problem with cypher systems is that they are invented by ingenious people, but in all cases so far, there have been just as clever people who have been able to break the cyphers. A cypher developed between just two people using what is called a one-time pad cypher is still almost impossible to break, but it's unusable once one needs to communicate with more than one person, and certainly unusable in commercial or government terms.

Unfortunately, RSA is now compromised, meaning that it is no longer safe. Indeed, there is already a method suggesting how it may be broken posted on the web, Google: "RSA compromised" if you're interested.

Of course, you don't get hordes of people shouting about it, as the longer the majority are not aware a cypher can be broken, the more those who wish to read encrypted messages can continue to do so. It is worrying though as all our financial transactions rely on RSA or derivatives such as PGP (Plenty Good Privacy) of this system.

So, if the present cypher system can be broken, where do we go from here? In my book 'The Shanghai Incident', I have suggested a method using WW2 technology along with lasers, but it would only be of use for governments and would not work with the current technology for commercial use. This novel also deals with the destruction of the Chinese hacking centre in Pudong area of Shanghai.

Now to look at why encryption is so important, quite *aside* from secret communications. PLC's and PCM's (programmable logic controllers and power control modules) are mini industrial computers built into almost all industrial machinery in order to control specific processes such as flight controls on an aeroplane, hospitals, dams, sewerage works, street lights, traffic lights, trains, vehicles of all types, (built after 1983), ships, generating stations, gas supplies, communications, nuclear power stations and many other things we take for granted.

Originally, PLC's were built into machinery to make it more efficient and to enable diagnostics to be carried out by skilled operatives. Some of the original PLC's codes were not even encrypted. With the advent of the internet, it was decided that instead of paying lots of maintenance teams, all these mini computers in static installations should be linked to the world-wide-web, thus saving large sums of money. It was a great idea, except by doing so, they are now all susceptible to hacking.

When you consider hacking, the thought is that a piece of machinery will simply be shut down, secrets read or data changed, but there is a greater danger. When Iran was trying to build an atomic bomb, they had thousands of centrifuges linked to the internet. The Americans broke in and rather than close them down, they instructed the internal PLC's to increase the speeds that exceeded the maker's safety barriers and thus they self-destructed. When the Iranians realised what was happening, they moved what was left underground and linked them together on their own circuit. A Mossad employee simply infected the system by using a flash drive. The program devised by the CIA was called Stuxnet. It took the Iranians about two years to recover. The message here is never allow anyone to put a flash drive into your computer as it could carry a virus, sometimes unbeknown to the owner of the flash drive.

Now, most equipment is encrypted and thus more difficult to break into, but once hacked, a simple instruction from a computer on the internet can cause havoc. Flash drives the size of a small coin can devastate a huge factory, and remember, a worm or virus introduced can destroy equipment instead of just shutting it down. Imagine a terrorist hacking into a train, disabling the braking system and increasing the speed to unacceptable levels.

The danger is about to become even greater. To decrypt a complicated cypher can take time, and in theory, in some scenarios, it could take a thousand years even using super computers. A normal PC can deal with about 65 thousand bits per second, but now we have the advent of the Quantum computer. A 50-qubit computer would be able to deal with 1,125 quadrillion bits per second. (A billion, billion). This means that it could decrypt any cypher or code in a split second. Because of the extraordinary power of these new machines that rely on quantum physics, it is almost certain that machines have been built with considerably more qubits than the 20 already admitted, but no country wishes to publicise the fact that they have such power. In fact Google have just announced that they have produced a Quantum computer that answered a question that a super computer would take ten thousand years to answer. It took just three seconds. Can you imagine if unregulated companies like Google can harness such power, where does that leave us?

This is the future, nothing will be safe. Even now, an expert with a laptop can break into any car made after 1983, and take control of it from outside by entering the vehicle's computer diagnostic system. The reason laptops were prevented from being taken into the cabin on airline flights, was due to the concern that they could be used to take control of an aircraft. We already know that hackers have been able to break into the US military systems, supposedly with the best computer defences in the world. Now we are handing the manufacturing of 5G phones to the Chinese, thus allowing them to create 'back-doors' which will enable them to harvest our data.

The thought is, that if you are not guilty of anything, it doesn't matter who reads your data or listens in to your telephone calls, but it will if your bank account is cleared out, your identity is stolen, your medical records are changed or scammers use your data to damage your reputation or steal money from you in other ways other than through your bank.

In the future, wars could effectively be won or lost within 24 hours, the winner being the country who has the fastest computer technology and the best defensive measures. Of course, defences will have to be built to counteract this digital threat; the best defence is for the recipient to send an electronic 'bomb' back to where the hacker is located and destroy the equipment used, (and maybe the hacker too) but we do not yet have this capability and indeed such an act may be too late anyway.

The other danger of those owning quantum computers, is the ability to capture data from all digitised sources including encrypted social media, and to use algorithms to create detailed preferences. Hugely useful for manipulating voters in national elections. The same data can be used to create 'fake news', which can create doubts about a particular politician, party or even another country.

We should not underestimate Corbyn and his ilk. Putin almost certainly managed to ensure the Trump campaign won in the USA. We have to assume that he would be minded to do the same here at some juncture. Imagine, if he was successful in helping to get the current socialist party elected with a majority, he would have achieved a situation where the UK would withdraw from NATO, reduce our defence spending and destroy our nuclear deterrent? Quite a prize.

Welcome to this brave new world!

2018

For Always

Jonathan Downes

When I was just a little boy of five my Godmother gave to me
a book about a river that flowed slowly to the sea.
I didn't realise then it was a deft allegory,
upon the stages of our life and our mortality.
It started in the mountains with a tiny silver spring,
the sacred fount of sustenance for every living thing,
but even at the age of five the magical thing for me,
was it was secure within itself and never ceased to be.

and you don't stop loving someone
    you won't stop loving someone
    you never stop loving someone
because somebody closed the door
and you don't stop loving someone
    you won't stop loving someone
    you never stop loving someone
just because they're not there anymore

The river was portrayed as self-aware, and as its waters flowed
on its journey from the source down to the mouth, its painted pages showed
fields and factories, and life and death, all the journeys on life's road,
until it dissipated in the sea, and then it shed its heavy load.
The last page of the book portrayed the river sad and wan,
as its story was now over and its journey had been done,
then the river realised it could revisit any part
of itself whenever it wanted, and it went back to the start.

and you don't stop loving someone
    you won't stop loving someone
    you never stop loving someone
because somebody closed the door
and you don't stop loving someone
    you won't stop loving someone
    you never stop loving someone
just because they're not there anymore

I have loved and lost and been bereaved, many that I've loved are gone,
leaving nothing now but memories of days when the sun shone,
and I remember the book about the river in that dark before the dawn,
and I realise if you remember them, then you never truly lose someone.
Because you cannot ever destroy energy, only have it change its form,
and we are all just massed electrons like the lightning in a storm,
and if those organised electrons are augmented with our love,

its an energy that can never end no matter what your thinking of.

and you don't stop loving someone
   you won't stop loving someone
   you never stop loving someone
because somebody closed the door
and you don't stop loving someone
   you won't stop loving someone
   you never stop loving someone
just because they're not there anymore

And love and life and death itself are not a mystery,
when you know that they're just phases of the way things have to be,
standing naked in front of the universe who knows what they will see,
but consciousness and love are energy and we know that will always be.
The laws of physics intimate that what I say is true,
that energy is pure and clean just like the way that I love you.
And though the universe is infinite, it's intimate as well,
and we occupy the spaces there where once the angels fell.

and you don't stop loving some
   you won't stop loving someone
   you never stop loving someone
because somebody closed the door
and you don't stop loving some
   you won't stop loving someone
   you never stop loving someone
just because they're not there anymore

The Postman Poet

Liz Shakespeare

"Edward Capern, 1819-1894, was nationally known as Devon's Postman Poet. Liz Shakespeare, the author of five books inspired by the history, the people and the landscapes of Devon, has written a novel which draws on historical research and Capern's own writing to tell the story of this extraordinary man's journey from obscurity to national renown, while capturing the opportunities and inequalities of the Victorian age. In the extract below, which forms the prologue to The Postman Poet, we meet Edward Capern as a successful poet before returning to his early life.'

Chapter One

Braunton, Devon, 1884

The secluded country station is tranquil in the late afternoon sunshine. The only sounds are the chirping of sparrows in the eaves and the murmur of voices from the group of gentlemen gathered on the platform, staring expectantly along the railway tracks that run across low-lying meadows.

After a few minutes a cloud of steam can be seen in the distance and as the engine comes into view a low roar is heard, drowning out all other sounds as the train approaches. When it hisses slowly to a standstill, just one carriage door opens and a stout man with a long white beard steps eagerly down on to the platform, followed by an elderly woman with two small children.

A gentleman steps forward. 'Edward, hello! How wonderful to see you back in Devon!'

The new arrival smiles broadly at the welcoming party. 'Thank you, thank you all! So many friends to greet us! This is a great day for me and a long-awaited one!'

He shakes hands warmly with each of them and then with the stationmaster hovering nearby, who looks rather taken aback at the unaccustomed familiarity.

'Welcome, Mr Capern. Can us take your bags for you, Sir?'

The lady holds on to the children's hands to restrain their excitement as the guard blows his whistle and the train wheezes and chuggs away from the platform. The four make their way out to the waiting cart for the last stage of their long journey, but the boy with the barrow who has been staring open-mouthed at the important passenger can contain his news no longer.

'Us used to learn your poems in school, Mr Capern, Sir.'

As the station cart creaked and swayed along the narrow lane, Edward contemplated the landscape he loved, and listened with pleasure to the children's chatter. He named the small village of Wrafton for them and pointed out the Manor Farm with its old cob linhays, then a brook that ran sparkling under the road bridge; he reassured his wife that in only a few more minutes they would arrive at their new home. As soon as the cart came to a halt and the horse stood patiently with downcast head, he rose and negotiated the steps without waiting for a hand from the driver. He landed heavily on his feet and gazed spellbound at his surroundings. The sun was low, shining on to the cottage windows and some little trees and fields, and now that the clopping of hooves had ceased, all was silent but for the rich, celebratory warbling of a thrush.

When he saw his favourite flowers growing in the hedge, Edward almost ran to them, cupped his hand around them and inhaled deeply.

'Janie! Primroses!'

His wife was standing in the cart waiting for the driver to help her down so he hurried over to his two grandchildren who had already clambered out.

'Look, Ilfra, Archie, primroses waiting for our arrival! Can you smell them?' He held out a flower to each obedient child. 'And there are bluebells and buttercups –' How good it was to be back in Devon! He flung out his arms excitedly while the horse jerked its head up in surprise.

'There's balm in the air, love, and bloom on the trees,
And warbling of woodlands, and humming of bees.'
'Never mind the poetry, Edward. Is this our new home?'

Jane was standing in the lane, staring up at the cottages. In the centre of the terrace stood a well-proportioned house, its porticoed entrance and sash windows looking down on the humble doorways and casements of the smaller dwellings. Edward hoped it would please her.

'It's not quite as grand as your drawing showed,' she said, 'but 'tis all the better for that. Look, children, here's the house Grandpa told us about, so no need to ask any more if we're nearly there.'

Ilfra went to lean against her grandmother's comforting side. 'And we're to live here with you and Grandpa forever?'

Jane met Edward's concerned glance before taking Ilfra's hand. 'Yes, chiel, you're to live here with us. See, Grandpa has the key so hold it between the two of you so's we can unlock our new door. There, you can go right on in, it's our home now, nobody else's.'

THE
POSTMAN
POET

Liz Shakespeare

The children rushed in but Edward paused on the doorstep. A rambling rose clambered up the porch to provide a canopy at the entrance; across the lane he could see the vegetable plot, a little neglected but of sufficient size to feed him and Jane and their two charges. The village would give them sanctuary, just as the lush hedgebank provided a haven for countless plants, birds and other creatures. In recent years such scenes had often featured in his dreams, as he imagined he strode again through narrow byways, greeting the flowers that had inspired his thoughts and the birds and brooks that lent him their melodies. The Devon lanes had been his greatest muse. Perhaps they would again prove generous. He shielded his eyes from the lowering sun. Away to the west a luminescence, suggestive of a large body of water invisible from where he stood, was drawn up into the sky. Devon!
He was home again, at last.

Later that evening, with the children finally settled in their makeshift beds and Jane resting in her chair, Edward stood at the window of the upstairs room that would become his library. The light was almost gone but as his gaze travelled over the panorama before him, he could still make out the silvery line of the river Taw below a sheltering shoulder of hills, Chanter's Folly towering above Appledore and the estuary of his beloved Torridge; then, between the rolling dunes of Braunton Burrows and the distant finger of Hartland Point, a narrow gleam which he knew to be the great ocean, where in daylight he would see stately ships gliding into the estuary to unload their cargoes on the quays at Fremington and Bideford.

Slowly, he turned his back to the window. The bookshelves he had described to the village carpenter had been fitted to two walls and seemed to be well-executed; they would do nicely. The trunks of books lay haphazardly where they had been placed with groans of relief by the removers. He had fretted about the trunks. If the weather was very wet they *must* be covered with oilcloth and he feared they would not be; the consequences of a drenching were too awful to consider. He got down painfully on to his knees, undid the clasp of the first trunk and lifted the lid. The books were a little shaken but appeared dry. He ran his hand over their covers; books bound in blue, brown and dark green cloth, books bound in leather with gold tooling and marbled edges, books with cracked spines and titles too faded to read; more than two thousand of them. Edward knew them all and loved them all; they were his companions, his inspiration.

He took one up and caressed it; this was the first of several given to him by his dear friend Elihu Burritt, and this, the first volume of poems by John Gregory with whom he had been friends since his early days in Bideford. These four lying side by side were all inscribed to him by their authors; and this one, this was his most treasured possession – *Antony and Octavius* by the great man Walter Savage Landor. He opened it reverently as he had hundreds of times to see the dedication, printed so every purchaser of the book could read it: '*These scenes are dedicated to Edward Capern, poet and day-labourer at Bideford, Devon.*' He sighed and replaced the book carefully in the trunk. Here was another – should this not have pride of place on his new shelves? It was a cheap edition of Bunyan's *Pilgrim's Progress*, its faded cover frayed at the edges, the spine broken and the pages loose, yet it was this very book that had opened his eyes to the world around him and set him on the path of poetry and learning, this book that had made him the man he was.

'*The Postman Poet* by Liz Shakespeare is published by Letterbox Books at £9.99

Also

The Poems of Edward Capern selected by Liz Shakespeare, Letterbox Books, £7.99
Both books are available from bookshops or from

www.lizshakespeare.co.uk '

Appledore Lifeboat

A hearty measure of Apple Brandy
A daring dash of Blue Curacao or creme de menthe
Top up with seafarer's pure lime juice
(to protect from scurvy)
Crushed ice (but avoid the icebergs)
and a chocolate curl floating on the surface
(to represent the lifeboat).

Who?

by Clothio

Who shall I sing my sad songs for if you are no longer here?
Who will catch me when I drunken fall with existence too heavy to bear?
Who will hold my hand in the tremulous gloom and kiss my weary eyes?
Ease back the vanguard of terrors unnamed, with gentle truths and little lies?

Who will lay quietly warm by my side, when Winter's wrath strides the hills
And slates are blessed with silver and spout and gutters trill,
To piccolo pipes of lead and iron that entice the chill water astray,
To a demonic dancing dark ocean, so many storm-swept miles away?

Who will you call when technology reneges on its promise of bright sound and light?
And who will plant in your darkness new stars, as only a lover might?
And who will attend when the labour pains come at the birth of a piercing scream?
As the claws of a nightmare snag at your soul, through the gauze of a curious dream?

Shall we never again guard the night-time when the wind in the sycamore cries,
And the owls melancholically calling that dares us to be none to wise.
As the moon wears a shroud in the branches and longing follows the fox
With hands on the church clock turning the key on shared memories box.

For what shall hold us together now whilst time's fragile fabric rips?
And the heart but collateral carrion, as the mask of rapacious reason slips.
And dreams petition bankrupt, and love no more than smoke
from the ashes of yesterday's passion and the glowing grey embers of hope.

Here I lay, still awake in the long small hours, swirling leaves talking low in the yard.
Tough as iron am I in my solitude now, strong but brittle, cold and unspeakably hard.
Like the Jurassic cliffs of endurance above a toothed and troubled shore,
I wait in the penumbra of patience, knowing who I await, as I must

…evermore.

SILK, SATIN AND A GOODNIGHT KISS

By CAPTAIN JAMES

I closed my eyes to block out the sunlight which streamed through the tall ward window. It was late autumn or perhaps early winter, I forget which. Time had lost a lot of meaning for me just then. I must say that the people here had been so very kind to me. After all it was their calling to be kind, but I knew that it would only be a matter of hours now before I would be free of their pipes and wires and computerised monitors. There would be some sadness at my passing I dare say but not much and that would not last long. About as long as it takes to digest the contents of my will. I would remember my few friends, that goes without saying and do my duty to what was left of my family such as it was. The little ones would get something of course. The others could go to the devil cursing me for a romantic old fool when they discovered that apart from a few gifts and mementoes everything would go to a girl I had not seen for 40, no, 50 years.

Time would have turned a quaint young lady into a quaint and probably crochety old one who, as I discovered long ago, cared for me not one iota, and could no doubt scarcely recall me now. How deeply and foolishly I loved her still, yet in our younger days she had wielded her indifference towards me like a blunt instrument. The bruises still hurt and I would extract a sweet revenge with my bequest and demonstrate my constancy at the same time.

Apart from a few minor things, small pictures, silver and so forth everything was to be turned into cash, except the houses which were to be rented out and she was to receive a pension for life of US$ 10,000 every month.

Even if she chose to give it away, as was likely, for her family were rather wealthy by the standard of her country, it would still be there in the post on the first of each month in a stark and perhaps cruel reminder that she could not possibly ignore of the injustice that lived and festered in the memory of an unwanted love. A love the echo of which would live and refuse to die long after I was gone.

The pain came and it went. How I longed to fall asleep. To rest in a long and blissful dreamless sleep. To be free from these insistent jangling mumbling voices which lurked like an incoherent crowd gathering on the fringes of my mind. What they signified I knew not but I confess to being bloody frightened. Rational thought told me it was just a side effect of the drugs. My emotion brushed this aside with intimations of an eternal hellish torment, condign punishment for my pomposity and literary arrogance.

I had lived by words and words would usher me into my grave and, God forbid, follow me beyond it. Do you wonder that I yearned for a sleep that would not come? A release and redemption. Not that I thought that likely. I sought some small respite in memories. Christmases, birthdays, holidays, and a mother's unconditional love. Invariably followed by fantasy lusts and lovers. Big breasts and short skirts. Bobbed hair, ponytails and turned up noses. Whichever route I took I always ended up thinking of her, my will, my death and the pension I had planned for her. None of which eased my mind in the slightest.

From God knows where came the memory of a walk in the park holding mother's hand while feeding the swans with stale bread. The trees were in full leaf and there were ducks as well as swans on the pond. I bent over to pick up a feather, black and blue tinged with white that gleamed in the sunshine. How fresh and clear are things at that age. Reason told me that I could have been no more than two or three at that time when all things are new and destined to stay in the heart for ever. I ran to show off my find as the vision collapsed and the voices started again. Louder and more insistent as they fought for the right to be heard. "Speak clearly curse you if you have something to say, say it." The pain came back with a rush. I thought that I might scream and as I bit down hard on the impulse fighting for breath, the ground beneath my hospice bed opened up and I fell into a deep dark hole. If I did scream with the shock of it, it was soundless as I plummeted down and down. If there was anything to see I never saw it.

The voices followed me down a piece but soon gave up as if not daring to follow. I may have forced my eyes open but if I did it was to no good purpose. I hung helplessly suspended in the blackest night it is possible for a sighted person to imagine. I had a feeling that I was falling but was unsure of even this until it began to lighten. How long I hung there slowly descending in that infernal twilight it is impossible to say; it might have been seconds or days. Slightly at first and then brighter and brighter, the light came back until with a sprawling crash I landed on something hard. It was a polished parquet wooden floor which smelled of lavender wax. What was this? Was it a memory? It had to be, but it was not. I tried to stand but could at first only crawl. The wooden floor gave way to a carpet. A red oriental carpet. I grasped the ornate leg of a table and pulled myself upright. The scale was all wrong. I could hardly see over the top. I pulled at the tablecloth but stopped when a plate or dish of some sort looked like it might crash down at any moment. Looking around I began to take in these strange surroundings. Everything was so pin sharp and in focus I knew that it had to be much more than a dream. I touched my face, but my glasses were absent. As was the stubble I had become so accustomed to of late. In fact, my chin was unnaturally soft but I gave the observation no mind just then. Whilst it was a room I had never been in before it all seemed strangely familiar. The smells of the floor polish and the coal in the brass scuttle.

There was coffee in the air and the sweet smell of roses in a green glass vase and the warm musty friendship of a leather book laying open on a low table, its yellow grey arms spread wide in an invitation to come inside and explore. A long case clock rang the half hour and brought its mellow tick to my attention. I knew without knowing, exactly how it would smell inside when its door was opened. I climbed up into a mountainous armchair and it too had its distinctive smell which was hard to pin down. Pipe tobacco perhaps. Yes pipe tobacco it was, and to prove my guess correct, on a small round table, in a small rack carved with nymphs and ivy, sat a row of pipes. Small, elegant thin ones which shone like new horse chestnuts. Fat black ones with curved stems and silver bands. A brown one which had once been white with a sculpted face upon the bowl. A stoneware jar and a box of matches. Catching sight of the matches reminded me of something from my childhood and I looked intensely at the hearth where the fire had been artfully laid with newspaper, kindling and small coals ready to burst into life at the hands of the parlour maid. Parlour maid? I never met a single person who could have afforded one. What did I know of rich Latakia, or meerschaum for that matter? These words popping into my mind uninvited.

I closed my mind eyes very hard and thought myself transported back to my sickbed. There was reason in this escapade somewhere. I had heard of dying men floating down tunnels to a white light and read something of out of body experiences, but this was different. Everything was so solid. So continuous. So unlike a dream.

It was so unlike my dreams anyway, with their taunting glimpses of an elusive and unrealised happiness with their complex opaque messages shifting back and forth in time and space. As long as I could remember my name, I was sure that could protect my sanity. I repeated my name over and over again, but even the sound of it began to feel stale upon my tongue. This would pass. Or would it? Would I awaken into my morbid bed and experience death in more than imagination? I shivered and felt the sting of tears for the first time in, oh so long. What if? What if it? ...the question refused to form up in my mind.

Whatever I was trying to put into words, faded as I became distracted by sounds in an adjacent room. They were girls' voices. Happy young voices, as light as thistledown carried on a warm summer breeze. They laughed over some whispered confidence or joke and I heard a heavy door closing. For a moment there was silence and then the music started. Diminuendo at first. Just someone lazily picking out notes on the keys with one hand. I walked on unsteady legs to the interconnecting doors, one of which was ajar and I stood in silence as the music started for real.

At a black grand piano, her back to me, sat a lady in a long white dress. I was drawn as though by a magnet. Silently I moved closer as the music grew louder. She was putting her heart into her practice. It was Chopin, but how I knew that, I have no idea. I have neither the knowledge nor the ear for music. A gentle breeze stirred the curtains by the French windows which opened onto the garden bringing with it the heavy cloying aroma of buddleia. But if I didn't care for its overdone perfume under normal circumstances it didn't bother me now. In fact I found that it added a further dimension to my mounting excitement. How can I describe the soft whiteness of that neck with its halo of golden downy hairs or the feet in those tiny satin slippers on the pedals or the thin forearms or the small thin fingers that danced over the keys? Had I gone though life in a blinkered rush never noticing such details, such as, the buttons on the back of her dress were iridescent mother of pearl and the weave of the fabric of the silk dress was simply loaded fit to burst, burst with a significance I could not explain in a thousand years? Had I ever seen such small ears or such petite fingernails? Oh what it must be to be her husband or her lover. Was a cruel providence to give me another final glimpse of pure contentment in a world that I could never ever have claimed as my own before the rampaging years had dragged me to the edge of the abyss?

It took all my courage to move as quickly and as quietly as I could to view this lovely creature in profile. Step by step. The notes of the music had a hard but not harsh quality I find so very difficult to describe. Crisp might be a better, but still, inadequate word. It was as though the notes had a tactile quality which elevated them above the mere vibrations of air. With just a little imagination one could touch their delightful waves as they passed by in majestic procession.

I could see her face clearly now and almost bit my lip in my excitement. It was her!

Was this the decomposing mind of a dying man playing tricks? It was her I tell you. Thrown into this tempest of sensation against all odds and against all logic.

How on earth could I ever imagine that this golden-haired ethereal musician could possibly be the embodiment of the dark feisty little goblin that had broken my heart almost half a century ago? It defined reason. But the whole experience was surreal. She caught sight of me and stopped playing for a moment to smile and made a gentle mue' with her lips. Was it my eyes that convinced me that they were in some way one and the same person? Whatever it was I was convinced of it. Her eyes were the loveliest cornflour blue beneath that blond fringe whilst "hers" were dark. Very slowly and very softly she began to play a different tune. The breeze bellowed the curtains beside the French windows and I could see out into the garden whose lawns ran down to a stream and beyond that fields of corn in stooks awaiting threshing. I recognised the tune immediately. It was a piece which had been on the programme of the last concert we had shared together before she slipped out of England and out of my life forever. Wagner had written this idyll as a lullaby for his new son Sigfried. Who was doing this impossible thing to destroy me utterly?

The prickly feeling in my eyes returned but this time I could not hold back the tears as incomprehension and sadness washed over me like a tidal wave and I began to cry. There seemed to be no end to my misery. Stout arms, which appeared out of nowhere, picked me up and carried me up stairs that creaked, wiped my face with a soapy flannel, eased me into a nightshirt and put me to bed.

"Now there's a good boy. Now you stop that fuss and mummy will be up to give you a goodnight kiss directly." The stair boards creaked in confirmation. "Why there she is now." She glided into the room in a rustle of satin bringing in her wake an air of utter calm. She bent over my little bed and in a cascade of golden hair kissed each of my salt laden eyelids. I stopped crying instantly and began to slip into the sort of deep, pain free, effortless sleep I had longed for, for so long.

The nurse drew the curtains and lit the gas light with a gentle pop then turned it low. An early moth fluttered against the shade.

As they left the nursery together I knew that whatever maelstrom of circumstance, time and space, might do to separate us, whatever form her body might take I would love this woman with all my heart forever. -

Reunion

By

P S Butler.

The vampire sunk his teeth into the soft, young flesh. He sucked the warm lifeblood from the girl, filling his mouth before swallowing. The ancient creature felt strength and vigour fill his veins. He dropped the girl and took a deep breath. Blood coated his teeth, and dripped from his chin. He viewed the other schoolgirls that lay nearby; it was nice to feast.

Edith Parker was more angry than worried. This term - more than any she could recall - was full of bad behaviour and rule breaking. The school was renowned for its good discipline, as well as its academic success. This trend could not be allowed to continue. She would have to make an example of the three missing girls!

Vargan was sated and felt strong again. In more recent decades he had appreciated the difference that young blood made to his body. In former days any blood would do, but there was certainly a different reaction now that many centuries had passed.

It was now gone midnight. Edith Parker, the Form Mistress, was furious. She would do her utmost - as ever - to keep this within her house. However, if she couldn't locate the errant 14-year-olds soon, though, she'd have to wake the headmistress, and the 'stuff' would really hit the fan. Edith decided to do one more round of the likely hiding haunts where 'young ladies' had got up to no good over all the years she had been at St Mary's. The year-dorm revealed three still untouched beds. The girls that were awake promised that they'd not seen, or heard, from Tori, Nikki and Nats since the evening meal, some five hours ago. Edith scoured the school by torchlight, not wishing to wake others with unnecessary illumination. The only signs of life had been some worryingly large rats in the cellar boiler room. Mr Mathers, the caretaker, would be informed in the morning. Only the three storey science block to check before Miss Sheringham would have to be informed.

Ground floor Physics was clear. First floor Chemistry also. Top floor Biology was unlikely as most girls weren't over-keen about skeletons, skulls and laboratory animals, even in daylight hours. She walked methodically between the benches, shining her lamp into all the dark corners. As expected, no sign of missing pupils. Edith stood at the large window, looking down upon the central courtyard area, perhaps hoping to see three shadowy figures tip-toeing across the flagstones. As she stood, the room seemed to become discernibly colder. The silence enveloped like a blanket. The scratchy noises of mice and rabbits and guinea pigs had stopped, but she felt, rather than heard, a slow breathing. The hairs on her neck and arms stood to attention as she scanned the room. She felt - rather than heard or saw - a presence. No noise or movement made her turn her eyes upwards.

The creature was laying against the ceiling, defying the laws of gravity. It was smiling at her. She stood paralysed as the vampire, Vargan, slowly lowered itself to the floor. He stood before her, still smiling. Edith could not move. She could see and breathe, but she couldn't move, and she could make no sound. The figure had black eyes. Black pupils, no irises. It smiled with unnaturally red lips. Full, fleshy lips. He took the torch from her grip and pointed the beam at the now open loft hatch. Edith registered the message, but she had become a terrified mute. He lifted her with one arm, as if she were made of straw, and they floated slowly up through the large hatch doors. On the floor of the roof space he illuminated the three naked schoolgirls. Her charges were blanched and lifeless. Worse still, somehow, were the smiles on their dead faces. Vargan turned Edith's head to face him. He smiled as he snapped her neck.

This would be a good reunion. The last coming together was in a small hill town in the Carpathians. Many of the residents, the foodstuff, had been old and infirm. Both tough skinned and no sport at all to catch. It was important to get the right ingredients, to set an appealing atmosphere. After all, the reunions were only once every 500 years. Vargan had found a good banqueting hall. The 'Ladies Only' college was set in a former stately home, set within its own parkland with views over a meandering river. The boarders numbered nearly 300, ranging from 11 - 18 years. Young, athletic and sweet. Three hundred English roses.

By two in the morning Miss Sheringham had made her own quick check for the three missing pupils *and* their form mistress. Lucy West, the Head Girl, had come banging on her door in floods of tears.

By four o'clock. the police had conducted what *they* called a thorough search of the college buildings, and were about to widen out into the grounds and nearby village.

All the while, the four corpses lay peacefully in the loft space of the Science Block.

June 30th dawned with a cloudless sky. Another 'scorcher' was predicted; the fourth day of the current heatwave. Six weeks has passed since the disappearance of the three boarders and their quondam form mistress, Mrs Parker. The whole area crawled with police and the media. No clues or signs had been found. All was scaled down. Apart from the appearance of the odd rogue, everyone was trying to carry on as normal.

On June 30th two 'bobbies' were stationed at the front gate; 400 yards from the main school building. There was no sign of any other members of officialdom anywhere in the school grounds. Four hundred and ten girls, boarders and local day scholars, and sixty-one members of staff continued with school activities as routinely as they could.

June 30th was Reunion Day. Exactly 500 years since a hill town in the Carpathians had been decimated and virtually wiped from the face of God's earth. Records suggested that nearly 1,300 men, women and children were slaughtered by 'flying demons'.

In stark contrast to what Hollywood would have us believe, vampires do not burn up in contact with sunlight. They prefer the dark, but so do many other creatures. So it was that the 63 remaining vampires of the Razinov Family flew unobserved into the woodland on the school estate. They arrived in the form of a congress of ravens, changing into human shape only once hidden by the fully leafed trees. Vargan was complimented on his find, even more so when dozens of teenage girls ran out onto the hockey pitches below.

Vargan suggested the feast should begin at 1.30. The girls and staff would have partaken of lunch and there would be a two hour window before it was time for the day pupils to go home.

The congress of ravens flew out of the trees and scattered to various points around the school, playing fields and perimeter locations. They landed on the sills of open windows. They perched at vantage points around the central courtyard, on the fences around the hockey pitches, and two ravens even alighted onto the railings close to the two policemen at the main gate.

Among a vampire's many attributes is telepathy. At 1.30 exactly, 63 vampires assumed human shape and attacked the school. They were inflamed with blood-lust. The policemen, Mr Mathers and the seven other male members of staff were killed outright within seconds - heads twisted and snapped from their bodies. Miss Sheringham, all female members of her staff and all the pupils were nothing but food and drink.

There are four possible outcomes from a vampire attack.

- An outright kill from violent trauma.
- Death from blood loss, both drunk and spilled.
- A blood drain from which one may survive.

- and the Hollywood favourite -

- The mixing of bodily fluids resulting in a new vampire.

Most fluid mixes are performed with young women, but a vampiress will only live for three centuries. A vampire may only fluid mix three times within its long life – usually two millennia, so it must choose its connections wisely, and at least one should be male if the family line is to continue.

The first ten minutes of the Reunion Day Feast were horrific slaughter. Teenage girls can move quickly, but no human can match the speed and strength of a vampire. These creatures can also change shape, defy gravity and mesmerise. The sheer terror of confrontation also instantly debilitates many of their victims. The telepathic strategy of the vampires, was to corral their victims into the central courtyard, but such was the unbridled savagery of many of the Razinovs that over half of the total number of females were ripped to death, or lay bleeding profusely from the tearing, slashing piercing fangs of their undead attackers.

The dead and the dying littered the schoolrooms, gymnasium, sport fields and courtyard. The sun burned down, no birds sang. Girls whimpered and prayed. The vampires lapped blood from their lips and chins, sucked blood from gushing necks and drank blood from opened wrists.

Miss Sheringham's last thought was to rue the rule that all mobile phones had to be turned off and handed in on entry to school premises. Contact with the rest of humanity was unlikely.

By two o'clock, 140 girls and women cowered in the courtyard. Their savaged friends and colleagues littered the red stained flagstones. The vampires stood sentinel around the arena. Tall, handsome, magnificent, terrifying, loathsome, blood-drenched vampires.

Molly Simpson trembled within the vestment chest in the Chapel. She, Verity and Jo had been hiding behind the lectern on the raised dais in front of the high altar when the first screams erupted. When a large dark figure had burst through the front door, Jo instinctively screamed and bolted towards the side fire exit. The figure was upon her in the blink of an eye. Molly and Verity clamped their hands to their mouths and watched with bulging, disbelieving eyes as Jo's screams were replaced with a wet chomping sound. Verity raced for the front door and, as the vampire spring after her, Molly slipped silently into the large chest. She tunnelled under the heavy garments and witnessed her best friends awful death through a small knot-hole. The tall, dark thing stood erect and scanned the chapel. She could hear it chewing with an open mouth.

Screaming, shouting and crying continued outside the chapel walls. The vampire walked towards the altar. Molly tried not to breathe, though her heart beat so loudly she was sure it would be heard. The monstrous figure got closer. She was sure it was looking directly at her through the little knot hole. Suddenly, it sprung to the left, almost out of vision, and roared a fearsome noise. It grabbed the large brass cross and hurled it, shattering the lovely St Mary's stained glass window. Then the horrifying sound of Jo gasping for breath. The vampire shot from view and Jo was silenced for the last time. The nightmare roared again and Molly watched, disbelieving of her own eyes, as it flew out of the splintered front door.

The noises were more distant now, the courtyard maybe, or at the front of the school? Molly reckoned she must have been in the box for a good 20 minutes. She was shuddering now with shock and fear. It felt very cold despite the heat of the day and the fact that she was covered over by many items of heavy clothing. The creature had not returned and she decided to emerge from her hiding place.

In the courtyard all became quiet. The tall monsters stood still. The women and children calmed, mesmerised. Vargan spoke. "Razimov Clan. It is good to commune. Long has it been, yet as if it were yesterday. The feast is good and not yet over. We will gorge ourselves and then depart to our homelands. Our next Reunion will be arranged by Brother Fanglon. Friends and family, let us eat and drink".

The spell was broken, the screaming started anew and the vampires attacked with intensity. Blood choked many girls, several were disembowelled. Necks were chewed through and limbs tossed into the melee as a charnel house game. Within short minutes the courtyard became an arena of death. A tangle of torsos, limbs, bones and ragged flesh. An army of of blood drenched undead friends.

Molly sneaked from the chapel door as the carnage began. She ran as fast as her twelve year old legs would carry her. She made the cover of the woods and fell exhausted into some brambles. The thorns ripped her legs and blood dripped from the criss-cross of scratches and cuts. She cried herself asleep and awoke as te congress of ravens flew noisily above her. Tears burned her eyes and flowed down her cheeks. Terrible images replaying in her imagination. The cawing birds had quietened now and it once more became very cold.

Molly looked up to see many large black birds in the branches immediately about her. She felt very afraid. A raven glid down from the branch above to land close by. As she stared it transformed into the vile creature she'd seen in the Chapel.

The monster knelt beside her and grinned. Its mouth was bloody and its breath was hot and sweet. She sat motionless and unable to make a sound as it bent and licked her wounds. Vargan raised his foul head to look into Molly's eyes. His eyes were black. Large black pupils, no irises. He smiled, a cold cruel smile and whispered "Welcome to the family". He stood tall, then began to float towards the branches above. The man-shape transformed once more to a large black raven which flew away.

Molly watch the congress of ravens disperse to the four winds. She was smiling but couldn't understand why!